MW00948283

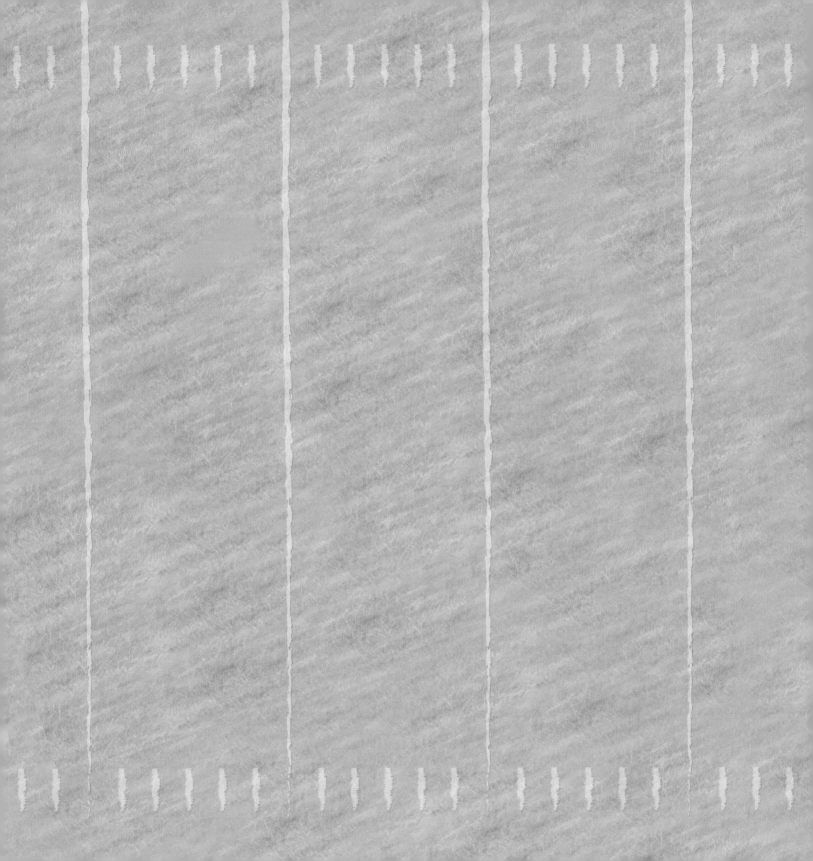

The Little Linebacker

Linebacker

A Story of Determination

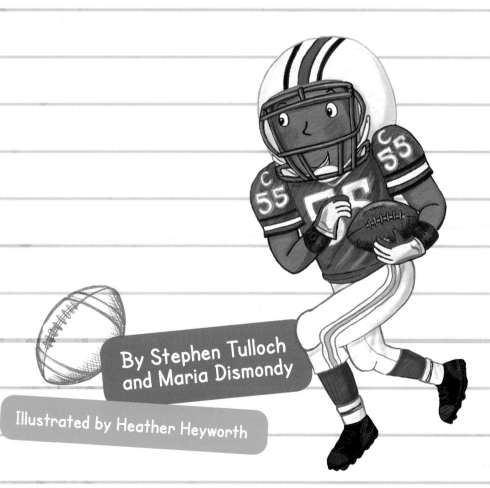

By Stephen Tulloch
and Maria Dismondy

Illustrated by Heather Heyworth

Copyright 2016 Stephen Tulloch and Maria Cini Dismondy
Illustrations by Heather Heyworth
Book Design by Maggie Villaume

First Printing 2016
All rights reserved.
Printed in the United States of America
Summary: Stephen is a little kid with big dreams of playing football. The odds are against him when he is tested and faced with challenges. This is a story of a boy who worked hard to defy the odds and become a leader.

Tulloch, Stephen (1985-)
Dismondy, Maria Cini (1978-)
The Little Linebacker: A Story of Determination
1. Courage 2. Character Traits 3. Bullying 4. Perseverance 5. Football 6. Empathy 7. Friendship 8. Determination 9. Diversity

ISBN: 978-0-9848558-4-1
Library of Congress Control Number: 2015912115

Cardinal Rule Press
An imprint of Maria Dismondy Inc.
5449 Sylvia
Dearborn Hgts, MI 48125
www.cardinalrulepress.com

This picture book biography of NFL player Stephen Tulloch includes inventive dialogue.

Before Reading

- Brainstorm with your child everything they know about the sport of football. This is called activating prior knowledge.
- Look at the pictures in the story. Make predictions about what might happen.
- Discuss the word determination. Give examples from your life to help your child understand the meaning of the word.

During Reading

- Stephen has a dream to become a professional football player in this story. Ask your child if they have a dream for their future-this helps them make a personal connection to the main character of the book.
- Stephen is faced with challenges in the story, but he never gives up. What character trait does Stephen possess?
- A mentor is someone who helps someone else learn something. Who was Stephen's mentor in the story? Do you have a mentor?

After Reading

- Stephen had a BIG dream for his future that came true. How did he make that happen?
- Using the fingers on your hand, retell the beginning, middle (describe three events), and end of the story.

More Learning

- Draw a picture of you living your dream in the future. Title it Dreams Do Come True.
- As an adult, Stephen gives back to schools and families through his foundation. List three things YOU can do to help others.
- Take your child to a local football game.

To my mom,
Mercedes Tulloch, thank you for always
believing in me when no one else did. I love you.
Thank you to my Aunt Selma and my two mentors
and father figures, Jay Lotspiech and Pepe Suarez.
Thank you for leading me in the right direction
and being positive role models in my life. —ST

To my parents, for teaching
me the value of kindness
and hard work! —MD

For the precious people in my life,
Willow, Laurie and my
mum Joyce, with love. —HH

Stephen ran in from the backyard to
find his mom bustling around the kitchen.
He was always outside playing with a football.
If he wasn't, he was daydreaming about being a professional
football player. Something REALLY BIG for a little kid to think
about and something that seemed possible only in his dreams.

As if his mom knew what he was thinking, she smiled and said, "Dream bigger dreams, Stephen." Tomorrow would be a big day. Stephen would go to his first Little League Football practice.

Stephen raced over to Coach Pep after practice. "Do we have practice again tomorrow, Coach?" he asked eagerly.

"Stephen, you have the energy of an entire football team! We only play once a week," the coach told him. "Come back and I'll teach you how to use that strength to play the game."

Stephen walked away, kicking the dirt. He was rarin' to go and didn't want to wait an entire week until his next practice.

Back at home, his mom said, "Learning something new takes time. Listen to your coach. You will pick it up. Remember, son, slow and steady wins the race," she added.

So Stephen came up with a plan. After school, he would round up his neighborhood friends to play football here, there, and everywhere! Then, when he played with his team, he would put his endless energy to work to win the game.

A few years later . . .

Stephen had to take a math test. He couldn't help but look outside and dream about the big game coming up. Before he could finish the test, the bell rang.

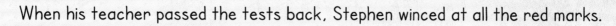

When his teacher passed the tests back, Stephen winced at all the red marks.

The girl next to him looked at his test and made a face. Maybe she thought he wasn't smart enough, Stephen worried. He knew the answers, but it was hard to focus. Like his mom always said, he *had* to keep his grades up to play football.

On weekends, Stephen's mom took him to work with her. He liked the nursing home, especially seeing Mr. Lotspiech, who Stephen looked up to. Mr. Lotspiech was there a lot visiting his mom. Stephen told him what happened at school.

Mr. Lotspiech patted him on the back. "A few bad grades are no reason to quit trying, Stephen. Study harder. Remember, practice makes perfect."

So Stephen studied harder.

Instead of playing card games the next few visits, Mr. Lotspiech quizzed him. Stephen had to work extra hard to focus and memorize the skills, but he did it.

During the next math test, a group of kids were playing flag football outside. But Stephen focused on the test instead.

Stephen's test came back with a much better score! "Hard work pays off," he whispered to himself.

A few years later . . .

Stephen was picked last for a team in his high school gym class. *This is crazy!* he considered. He had been playing football for ten years now, and he played well. He wanted to be chosen first so he could lead the defense.

Stephen's best friend John looked at him. "What's wrong?"

"I was picked last. I'm not going to play."

John pulled Stephen aside. "Man, *that* isn't a reason to give up the game. Keep playing and be part of the team. Remember, sticks in a bundle are unbreakable."

So Stephen kept playing.
He wasn't always chosen first and
didn't always play the position he wanted.
But he was a good teammate, and it made him a
better player.

A few years later . . .

Stephen sat in the locker room after a big win for his college team. He overheard some scouts talking about him. "He's undersized and won't make it in the pros." Stephen felt as if he had been hit with a ton of bricks. He looked up at a poster next to his locker.

YOU CAN. YOU WILL. END OF STORY.

Stephen had played the game long enough to *believe* that anything was possible for him. He could and he would. End of story.

In a loud, crowd-filled stadium with his mom in the stands, Stephen, captain of the defense, called the play and his teammates lined up. When the ball was thrown, Stephen intercepted it and ran it in for a touchdown.

The crowd went wild. Stephen was the star of the game.

Stephen made his dreams come true. He worked hard. He studied hard. He was part of the team. And he never stopped believing in himself.

Today, thanks to the love and support of his mom, Mr. Lotspiech, and friends along the way, Stephen inspires others to "dream bigger dreams." He uses his good fortune to pay it forward to other children and families.

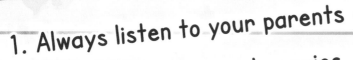

Tully's Tips for Kids

1. Always listen to your parents

2. Eat your fruits and veggies

3. Study hard in school

4. Be a good teammate

5. Never give up

6. Hard work pays off

1997

Tennessee Titans 2006-2010
Detroit Lions 2011-2016

The Stephen Tulloch Foundation:
This foundation helps assist underprivileged youth with opportunities to be successful. Mr. Tulloch's goal is to supply youth with the essentials to build self-esteem, establish their goals, and help unlock their potential.

Operation 55:
This program has helped hundreds of children and families across the Metro Detroit area during the holidays by adopting families affected by cancer. Operation 55 provides dental care for kids without health insurance, promotes educational projects across Detroit, and hosts free activities and camps for youth in Detroit and Miami.

http://www.tulloch55.com

Stephen Tulloch just finished his 10th season in the NFL as a middle linebacker. He has played for the Detroit Lions and Tennessee Titans. Tulloch was drafted in the 4th round of the 2006 NFL draft out of North Carolina State University. He launched the Stephen Tulloch Foundation in 2009 and has helped thousands of people through his community outreach and generous giving. Tulloch was named as one of the top 100 players in the NFL in 2012 & 2013, has been selected as a team captain of the Detroit Lions by his teammates and has been awarded multiple awards nationally and locally for his efforts off the field including the Walter Payton Man of the Year Award, The Robert Porcher Man of the Year Award, the Grid Iron Great Award along with the NFLPA PULSE award and being a finalist for the Byron "Whizzer" White Award which recognizes the top foundations in the NFL. Stephen was born and raised in Miami, where he still resides in the off-season with his dogs, Nash & Mia.

Maria Dismondy is an award-winning author, specializing in books about challenges children face. A topic close to her heart, Maria's own childhood experience inspired her first book, *Spaghetti in a Hotdog Bun*. Seven books later, Maria's commitment to empowering children with courage and confidence has reached new heights, touching the hearts and hands of children the world over. Maria's latest book, *The Little Linebacker*, drives home the important message that hard work and dedication can pay off. Dreams really can come true! As a sought-after speaker, Maria spreads her message by presenting at schools and conferences across the country. She holds degrees in education and child development. Maria lives in southeastern Michigan with her husband, Dave, and their three book-loving children.

Heather Heyworth lives and works in a sleepy Suffolk market town in the UK. After graduating from Goldsmiths College, London University, with a higher diploma in art and design, she went on to become creative manager within a busy design studio and then art editor at a large greeting card publisher. While her two children were small she designed greeting cards, giftwrap, calendars, plush toys, and packaging on a freelance basis. Her introduction into the world of children's books started with illustrating, designing, and co-publishing her own licensed character activity books. She wrote and illustrated her first picture book in 2009. To date she has illustrated many books including picture, board and educational books. From an early age she has had a passion for illustration and can't imagine doing anything else.